To my brother
Jimmy
J. B.

First published by Candlewick Press

C P

CANDLEWICK PRESS
2067 MASSACHUSETTS AVENUE
CAMBRIDGE MA 02140

ISBN 0-590-99286-4

Text copyright © 1996 by Sam McBratney.
Illustrations copyright © 1996 by Jill Barton.
All rights reserved. Published by Scholastic Inc., 555 Broadway, New York, NY 10012,
by arrangement with Candlewick Press.

12 11 10 9 8   1/0

Printed in the U.S.A.

First Scholastic printing, November 1996

The pictures were done in pencil and watercolor.

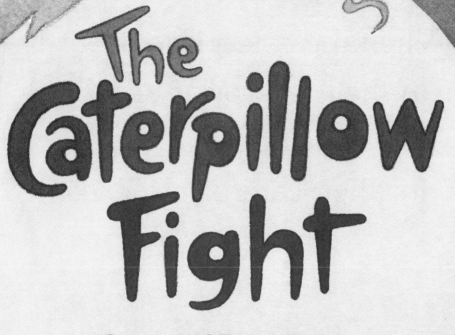

The Caterpillow Fight

SAM McBRATNEY

ILLUSTRATED BY
JILL BARTON

CANDLEWICK PRESS
CAMBRIDGE, MASSACHUSETTS

When the caterpillars went
to their caterpillar beds,
They all had caterpillows
for their caterpillar heads.

One naughty caterpillar,
  in the middle of the night,
Woke the other caterpillars
  for a caterpillow fight.

Two little caterpillars
gave caterpillow blows
To another caterpillar
on her caterpillar nose.

The tallest caterpillar,
  from her caterpillar height,
Brought down her caterpillow
  with all her caterpillar might.

The other caterpillars,
hiding down below,
Watched the caterpillow
feathers fall like
caterpillow snow.

There were caterpillow thumps
and caterpillow whacks
On caterpillar tummies and
on caterpillar backs.
The caterpillar laughter
and the caterpillar din
Went on and on and on until . . .

"Stop all this silly nonsense,
    I can hardly hear my ears.
This caterpillar laughing
    will end in caterpillar tears!"

Now when the caterpillars go
to their caterpillar beds,

There's just one *l-o-n-g* caterpillow
for all those caterpillar heads!